Aloha Bear

the
FOOtPRiNt
Detective

To Souhei Kalani, with aloha

ISLAND HERITAGE

Aloha Bear wakes up from a nap feeling all empty in the tummy.

"Time for a snack!" he says.

"Uh-oh, my guava jelly sandwich is gone!" cries Aloha Bear.

"Look at all these footprints! Who hid my sandwich?"

Can you be a footprint detective and find Aloha Bear's sandwich?

Aloha Bear follows the dotted lines in the sand. He stops and says, "Did you see my sandwich?"

"Maybe the bird hid my sandwich."
Aloha Bear climbs up the palm tree.

Aloha Bear hears a loud chit-chat noise.
He runs behind the low bushes.
"Excuuuse me!" shouts Aloha Bear.

Shhh...Gecko is taking a

8

"Where did my sandwich go?" sighs Aloha Bear as he tries to sit down.

Just then, a voice says, "Wait! Don't sit on us, please."

"Who is singing that beautiful song?" says Aloha Bear.
He follows the song and footprints.
"I just wonder," he asks, "if you saw my sandwich?"

"I smell food," says Aloha Bear, sniffing.
"Could it possibly be...?"

"I am so hungry," says Aloha Bear as his tummy growls. Then, he hears a soft voice calling, "Aloha Bear, Aloha Bear...," from behind the sand castle.

"These footprints look suspicious!" says Aloha Bear as he rushes behind the beach chair.

"Something smells yummy," say the animals as they follow the smell (and footprints)!

Do you remember who made these footprints?